APARTMENT 4A

D0987660

OUT OF CONTROL

Book 2

PJ Gray

SADDLEBACK
PUBLISHING
www.sdlback.com

APARTMENT 4A

APARTMENT 4A: BOOK 1

OUT OF CONTROL: BOOK 2

DEAD HELP: BOOK 3

SADDLEBACK
PUBLISHING
www.sdlback.com

Copyright ©2014 by Saddleback Educational Publishing

ISBN-13: 978-1-62250-709-2
ISBN-10: 1-62250-709-6
eBook: 978-1-61247-960-6

Printed in Guangzhou, China
NOR/0913/CA21301743

18 17 16 15 14   1 2 3 4 5

AUTHOR ACKNOWLEDGEMENTS

I wish to thank Carol Senderowitz
for her friendship and belief in my abilities.
Additional thanks and gratitude to my family and
friends for their love and support; likewise to the
staff at Saddleback Educational Publishing for
their generosity, graciousness, and enthusiasm.
Most importantly, my heartfelt thanks to
Scott Drawe for his love and support.

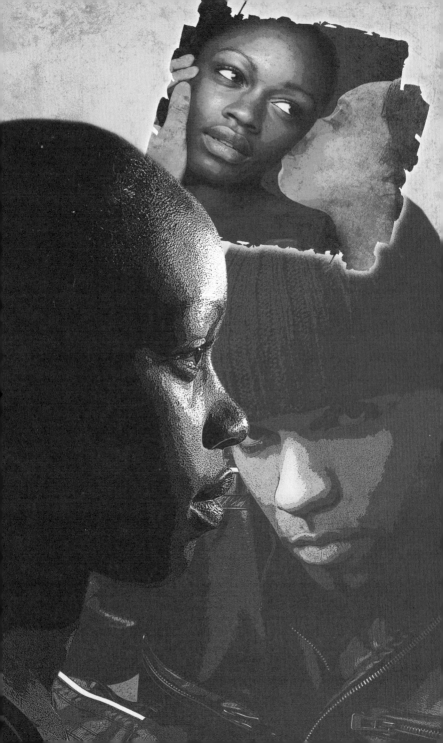

HER MOTHER

Bree saw the ghost of her mother in apartment 4A. "They call me Tutu," the ghost said. Tutu was her mother's nickname. Then the ghost jumped out the window.

Bree wanted to see her mother again. She had so many things to ask her.

Bree lived with her aunt in apartment 4B. Her brother, Andre, spent more time on the street. He only came home looking for money.

Bree's aunt was getting sicker. She stopped getting out of bed. Her aunt did not want to see a doctor. "Leave me alone," her aunt would say.

Bree was getting ready for work. She heard a key open the front door. Andre entered and walked slowly to her. Bree knew he wanted money. He was looking for his aunt's monthly check.

"Did you cash her check?" Andre asked.

"No. It wasn't in the mail. It must be late again," Bree replied.

Andre pulled out his knife and stood close to her. "I know you got a job. Who're you working for?" he asked.

"I don't have a job. I'm still looking," Bree lied. She tried to be strong.

Bree had some money in her coat pocket. The rest of her money was in her shoe in the closet. "I'll give you some money," Bree said. "First I want to ask you about our mother."

"Give me the money," Andre said. He put the knife to her face. She could smell the booze on him.

Bree pulled the money from her pocket. Andre grabbed it. "Where's the rest of it?"

"That's it," Bree replied. "Get out! Now!"

Andre left apartment 4B. Bree waited to leave. She was late to work that day.

INSIDE THE BOX

Bree went to the mailbox in the lobby. Her aunt's monthly check was not there. There was a letter in the mailbox. It was from the landlord.

The letter said he wanted the back rent. It also said he would be in town soon. He wanted to kick them out of apartment 4B.

Bree went to work. She hoped to get a delivery job. She hated the work. But she needed the money.

Her boss, Mr. Edwin, was at his desk. "Take this box," he said. "Take it to three forty-nine Pine Street."

"Okay," Bree replied. "Yes, sir."

"But wait until it gets dark," he added. Mr. Edwin stood up from his chair. "Did anybody see you when you made the other deliveries?"

"No. Nobody. I promise," Bree replied.

"Good," Mr. Edwin said. "Put the box in the trash can. Same as before."

Bree could see the gun under his coat.

Bree had to know what was in the box. She took it home. Her aunt was asleep in the bedroom. Bree closed the bedroom door. She put the box on the sofa.

Bree slowly pulled the tape from the box. It was hard to peel off. She carefully opened the top of the box. Bree was shocked. The box was filled with drugs.

At that moment, Bree could hear a cry from apartment 4A. It was Tutu. It was the ghost of her mother.

DARK DELIVERY

It was getting dark outside. Bree sat on the sofa with the box of drugs. She had to deliver it soon. She could hear the ghost of her mother crying in apartment 4A. Bree wanted to see Tutu, but she had to leave.

Bree carefully resealed the box. She took the bus to 349 Pine Street. Bree sat on the bus with the box on her lap. She was scared. She wondered if Mona knew about the box. The drugs. The gun. "Does Mona deal drugs too?" Bree asked herself.

She left the bus and walked to Pine Street. It was dark now. There was only one street light at the end of the block. The buildings were empty.

Bree put the box in the trash can at 349 Pine Street. She heard a sound from the street. She looked around. There was a man next to an old car at the end of the block. It looked like her brother. Was it Andre?

Bree ran to the other side of the building. She did not want to be seen. She knew she was in danger.

She ran as fast as she could. She ran behind other buildings and down other streets. She did not see anyone following her. She was hot. And breathing fast. Her heart pounded.

Bree took the bus back home. Her aunt was asleep.

Bree sat on the sofa in the living room. She could not sleep. She waited. She waited for her brother. She waited. She waited to hear the sound of her mother's ghost from apartment 4A.

REMEMBER ME

Bree was awake most of the night. She waited to hear a cry from next door. Bree was very tired. She began to fall asleep, then she heard a sound. It was her mother's ghost in apartment 4A. It was Tutu.

Bree jumped from the sofa and ran to the door. She ran across the hall to the front door of apartment 4A. The door was always open when she heard the ghost. This time the door was closed.

"No!" Bree yelled as she turned the knob. "Why's the door locked? Open the door!"

"My poor baby needs help," the ghost cried.

"Please unlock it, Tutu!" Bree cried. "It's me. It's Bree!"

Tutu's ghost stopped crying. Bree could hear nothing from inside the apartment. "Tutu, are you there?" Bree asked. "Open the door! I must see you!"

Bree looked at the knob. She put her hand on it one more time. She turned it. The door opened. Bree ran into apartment 4A. It was empty.

Bree fell to the floor and began to cry.
"Where are you?" she said to herself.

Suddenly, Bree felt a cold wind in the room.
She looked at the window. It was closed.
Bree turned around and saw Tutu, the ghost
of her mother.

"My poor baby needs help," Tutu said.

"It's me, Mama. It's Bree. Don't you
remember me?" Bree cried out.

Tutu looked at Bree and said nothing. "Andre doesn't need your help!" Bree cried out. "I need your help!"

The ghost of Tutu turned and melted into the wall. She was gone.

Bree sat on the floor of apartment 4A. She sat there for the rest of the night.

LUNCHTIME SECRET

Bree knew her boss was dealing drugs. Bree needed the money from her job. But she wanted to quit. Bree needed to talk to Mona, her only friend.

"I want to take you to lunch," Bree said. "Can you come?"

"Sure I will," Mona replied. "I never turn down lunch."

Bree smiled. Bree could not afford to buy a big lunch for Mona. But she had to talk to her. Bree and Mona walked to the hot dog stand next door. They sat down to eat.

"I have to tell you something," Bree said.

"You look upset," Mona replied. "What is it?"

"Those boxes that I deliver for Mr. Edwin," Bree said.

"What about them?"

"They're filled with drugs."

Mona looked at Bree. She frowned. Then Mona looked down at her food. "I don't want to know about it," Mona said.

"I had to tell somebody," Bree replied. "You're my only friend. I trust you."

"Bree, I have kids to take care of," Mona said. "I have to keep this job."

"I know," Bree said.

"I don't want to know about this," Mona said. She got up and walked away.

"But you're in danger too."

Bree saw Mona walk back to the office. She sat at the table looking at her lunch. She could not eat.

LAST WORDS

Bree came home from work. Mr. Edwin gave her no delivery jobs that day. She needed more money. She knew her brother would come back. Bree did not know why he wanted more money. Was it for booze? Was it for drugs?

Bree saw her aunt in bed. Her aunt was very sick. She would not see a doctor. Bree sat on the end of the bed.

"I need to ask you about my mother," Bree said.

"Leave that alone," her aunt replied.

"No. Tell me about my mom. Tell me about your sister. Please."

"My sister was a good girl," her aunt said. "She liked to dance around the house. That's why we called her Tutu."

Bree had never heard this story before.

"Then Tutu got with a bad crowd. Things got bad," her aunt said.

"Who was my father?"

"Tutu didn't know your father," her aunt replied. "She didn't know Andre's father."

Bree had never heard this before. She never knew her brother had a different father. Her half brother.

Bree's aunt closed her eyes. "I'm so tired," her aunt said.

"How did Tutu die?" Bree asked. She moved closer to her aunt.

"My head hurts," her aunt said. "Go away."

"I need to know," Bree said. "Please. I need to know!"

Her aunt said something Bree could not hear.

"What did you say?" Bree asked.

"She jumped," her aunt said softly.

"What do you mean? Jumped? Tell me!"

Her aunt's mouth stopped moving. Her face turned pale. She was dead.

NEVER COME BACK

Bree sat on the edge of her aunt's bed. It was dusk. The room was dark. Her aunt was dead. Bree was thinking about her aunt's last words. Bree was thinking about Tutu, her mother.

Just then, Andre unlocked the front door. He saw Bree in the bedroom.

"She's dead," Bree said to her brother. "She just died. We need to call the police." Bree got up and walked to the phone.

"No!" Andre said as he grabbed her arm. "No police. Nobody can know."

"Why?" Bree asked. "We didn't kill her."

"What about her monthly checks?" he asked. "If people know she's dead, her money stops coming."

"Stop it!" Bree said. She pushed away from him. "We have to tell somebody." Bree started to cry.

"No!" Andre grabbed her arm. He put his knife to her face. "I'll take care of this."

"What are you going to do?" Bree asked.

"I'll take care of this," Andre said. "Don't tell anyone." He let go of her arm. "Now get out of here," he said.

Bree ran out of apartment 4B. She stood in the hall. She ran to the front door of apartment 4A. She turned the knob. It was locked.

Bree ran to the end of the hall and opened the window. She stepped onto the old fire escape. This time she was not afraid and did not get dizzy. She did not care. She opened the stuck window. And she went in apartment 4A.

"Where are you, Tutu?" Bree called out. The apartment was empty. "Where are you, Mama? I need your help!"

Bree sat on the floor. She stayed there for the rest of the night. She waited for Tutu, but Tutu never came.

GET THE JOB DONE

Bree woke up on the floor of apartment 4A. She was afraid to go back to apartment 4B. Was her dead aunt still there? Was Andre still there?

Bree opened the front door of apartment 4B and walked in. Her aunt's body was gone. Andre was gone. Bree looked at the living room floor. The big rug was gone too.

"He wrapped her body in it," Bree said to herself. Bree did not want to be there. She got ready for work and left. For the first time, Bree was happy to go to work.

Bree got on the bus. She sat and wondered how she could leave town. She wondered if she would have enough money. Where would she go?

She opened the office door and saw Mona at her desk. Mona did not want to talk to her.

Mr. Edwin gave Bree a new delivery job. She had to take another box to Pine Street.

Bree took the bus to Pine Street and found the same trash can. She was not scared. She just wanted the job done. She wanted to get away.

Bree put the box in the trash can. Then she heard a shot. A second shot hit the wall next to her. Bree fell to the ground and waited.

Bree got up and ran around the corner. She looked back. Then she ran behind another building. Bree ran down an alley. Then another. She ran down three more alleys until she stopped. She was scared.

Bree got on a bus and went home. She knew she had to get out of town. She knew she could not tell Mr. Edwin about the gunshots. If he knew, he would never give her another delivery job. If he knew, he might hurt her. She needed the money so she could leave town for good.

ONE LAST JOB

Bree went to work the next day. "One last job and I'm out of here," Bree said to herself.

Mona would still not talk to Bree. Mr. Edwin gave Bree another delivery job at the end of the day. Bree had to take another box to the same building on Pine Street.

"Don't put it in the trash can," Mr. Erwin said. "Open the back door. Put it inside."

Bree got to the building on Pine Street. It was dark now. Bree looked around for somebody. She did not see a single person. Bree tried to open the back door, but it was locked. She knew she had to get the box inside.

Bree saw a window by the door and opened it. She went inside the empty building and put the box on the floor.

"What's in the box?" said a dark shadow. Bree turned. It was Andre. He walked slowly to her. "Give me the box," he said. He had his knife in his hand. Bree picked up the box from the floor.

"What are you doing here?" Bree asked.

"Give me the box now. Then I won't hurt you," he said.

"I will, but only if you tell me two things," Bree replied.

"No deal," Andre said as he walked closer. "Give it to me."

"Where did you take our aunt's body?" Bree asked.

"Why do you care?" Andre said. "I took care of it."

"How did our mother die? I want to know."

"Why? She was a drunk like me. She killed herself."

"How did she do it?" Bree asked. "Where? When?"

Andre just stood there. He said nothing.

"Tell me. Then I'll give you the box," Bree said.

JUMPER

Andre sighed. He put his knife away. He did not want to tell Bree. But she needed to know.

"We lived across the hall," Andre said.

"Wait," Bree replied. "You mean in apartment 4A?"

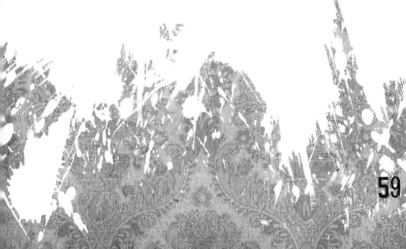

"Yes. You were a baby, and I was a kid," he said. "One night you were crying. I woke up."

"What happened?"

"Mama was drunk. Mad at us," Andre said softly. "She hit you, then me. She hit me hard. Then she jumped."

"Jumped out the window?" Bree asked.

"Yes," Andre said softly. "I ran to the window. I saw her on the ground. She was dead."

"I saw her too," Bree replied. "I saw her in apartment 4A."

"What? What are you talking about?"

Suddenly, they heard a click. It was the clicking sound of a gun. Bree turned and saw a shadow. Holding a gun.

ABOUT THE AUTHOR

PJ Gray is a versatile, award-winning freelance writer experienced in short stories, essays, and feature writing. He is a former managing editor for *Pride* magazine, a ghost writer, blogger, researcher, food writer, and cookbook author. He currently resides in Chicago, Illinois. For more information about PJ Gray, go to www.pjgray.com.